THEN AND NOW
COOKING
THEN AND NOW

by Nadia Higgins

pogo

Ideas for Parents and Teachers

Pogo Books let children practice reading informational text while introducing them to nonfiction features such as headings, labels, sidebars, maps, and diagrams, as well as a table of contents, glossary, and index.

Carefully leveled text with a strong photo match offers early fluent readers the support they need to succeed.

Before Reading

- "Walk" through the book and point out the various nonfiction features. Ask the student what purpose each feature serves.
- Look at the glossary together. Read and discuss the words.

Read the Book

- Have the child read the book independently.
- Invite him or her to list questions that arise from reading.

After Reading

- Discuss the child's questions. Talk about how he or she might find answers to those questions.
- Prompt the child to think more. Ask: There are many ways to prepare and cook food. How do you cook your favorite foods?

Pogo Books are published by Jump!
5357 Penn Avenue South
Minneapolis, MN 55419
www.jumplibrary.com

Library of Congress Cataloging-in-Publication Data

Names: Higgins, Nadia, author.
Title: Cooking then and now / by Nadia Higgins.
Description: Minneapolis, MN : Jump!, Inc., [2019]
"Pogo Books are published by Jump!"
Audience: Ages 7-10. | Includes index.
Identifiers: LCCN 2018034352 (print)
LCCN 2018035655 (ebook)
ISBN 9781641284738 (ebook)
ISBN 9781641284714 (hardcover : alk. paper)
ISBN 9781641284721 (pbk.)
Subjects: LCSH: Food—History—Juvenile literature.
Cooking—History—Juvenile literature.
Classification: LCC TX355 (ebook)
LCC TX355 .H48798 2019 (print) | DDC 641.3009—dc23
LC record available at https://lccn.loc.gov/2018034352

Editor: Jenna Trnka
Designer: Molly Ballanger

Photo Credits: Lighttraveler/Shutterstock, cover (slow cooker); Suzanne Tucker/Shutterstock, cover (chicken); Weerachai Khamfu/Shutterstock, cover (flames); xpixel/Shutterstock, cover (logs); mama_mia/Shutterstock, 1; goir/Shutterstock, 3; SolStock/iStock, 4; Library of Congress/Getty, 5; AS Food studio/Shutterstock, 6-7; Cath Harries/Alamy, 8-9; B Christopher/Alamy, 10 (left); walterericsy/Shutterstock, 10 (right); ClassicStock/Alamy, 11; apomares/iStock, 12; American Stock Archive/Getty, 12-13; Steven Gottlieb/Getty, 14-15; Stephen Saks Photography/Alamy, 16; ClassicStock/Getty, 17; Hemant Mehta/Getty, 18-19; Sergey Yechikov/Shutterstock, 20-21; Dave_Pot/iStock, 23.

Printed in the United States of America at Corporate Graphics in North Mankato, Minnesota.

TABLE OF CONTENTS

CHAPTER 1

COOKING IN THE PAST

Chop. Boil. Stir. Add spices. How do you cook? Meals today are much different than those in the past. So are the ways we cook them.

Long ago, Native Americans found food in the wild. They gathered berries and nuts. They hunted animals. They cooked food over open fires. Or on hot stones. Where do we get our food today? And how do we cook it?

In the 1700s, **colonial** Americans grew food. Corn. Squash. Carrots. Apples. They raised animals for meat. They milked cows. Everything was made from scratch. Butter. Even bread.

Food was fresh. But it **spoiled** fast. So people dried vegetables. And they salted meat. These methods helped **preserve** food.

DID YOU KNOW?

White settlers learned about corn from Native Americans. Corn became the most important food in early America. People used it for bread, pancakes, mush, and stew. Corn also fed farm animals.

deli

In the 1800s, many **immigrants** came to the United States. They brought their **cultures**. That also meant new foods and ways of cooking. These new Americans opened the first **delis**. Restaurants. Grocery stores.

TAKE A LOOK!

You can thank immigrants for many dishes we enjoy today!

GERMAN
hot dogs and hamburgers — 1870s

JEWISH
bagels — 1880s

ITALIAN
pizza — 1900s

CHINESE
egg rolls — 1930s

MEXICAN
nachos — 1940s

JAPANESE
sushi — 1970s

MIDDLE EASTERN
hummus — 2000s

CHAPTER 2

FASTER AND EASIER

Food was once limited. People ate what was grown nearby. That changed in the late 1800s. **Canned** food kept food preserved for years. We still can food today.

icebox

At home, cooking got easier, too. Gas ovens replaced fires. Milk was delivered right to the door. The family's **icebox** kept it cold.

Cities grew in the early 1900s. People worked in factories instead of on farms. Factory machines helped make and package food. Like what? Candy. Soda. Chips. These **processed** foods were tasty and cheap. Food **brands** like Hershey's, Cheetos, and Coca-Cola became famous.

1910s
Coca-Cola

Coca-Cola factory

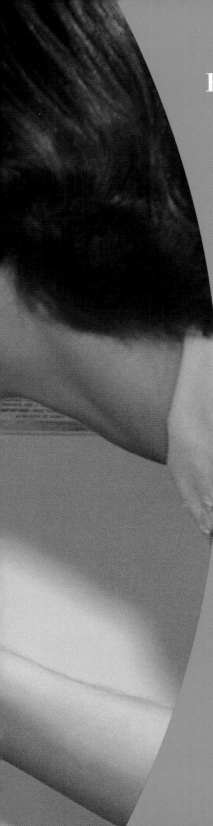

By the 1950s, kitchens changed again. Now there was **electricity**. Refrigerators. Freezers.

People also didn't have to spend hours cooking. They could buy frozen TV dinners at the grocery store. These came in trays that went straight into the oven. For dessert? A cake whipped up from a boxed mix instead of from scratch.

WHAT DO YOU THINK?

Does your family buy frozen meals? Or does your family cook from scratch more often? Which way of cooking do you prefer? Why?

CHAPTER 3

CHOOSE YOUR FOOD

In the 1970s, more women worked outside of their homes. Families were busier. Who would make family dinner now? Fast-food restaurants. Here, dinner came cheap. And without shopping, cooking, or washing dishes!

But fast foods were processed and unhealthy. Making them was hard on the environment. The health food movement started. People started buying natural, **organic** foods.

In the 1980s, cooking shows took off. TV chefs showed each step to making a fancy meal. Some people loved the challenge of **gourmet** cooking.

Microwave ovens entered home kitchens. Frozen meals could be ready in just a few minutes. We still use microwaves for cooking today.

WHAT DO YOU THINK?

What things does your family think about when choosing food? Taste? Health? Cost? Do these determine what your family buys?

microwave

slow
cooker

Today, we have many food choices.
And more ways to cook our food.
A slow cooker cooks food at
a low temperature for hours.
Instant Pots pressure cook foods.
They speed up cooking so your
family can spend time doing
other activities.

How do you like to cook?
Do you have favorite recipes?
Search for one online.
Watch a cooking video.
What will you try next?

ACTIVITIES & TOOLS

MAKE YOUR OWN BUTTER

Long ago, people used a butter churn to turn cream into butter. This device shook up the cream until it hardened. You can make your own butter using just a jar.

What You Need:
- jar that fits nicely in your hand
- heavy cream (enough to fill the jar halfway)
- bowl
- cold water

① Fill the jar halfway with heavy cream. Screw the lid on tight.

② Shake the jar as hard as you can. The cream should slosh against the top and bottom of the jar.

③ After a couple minutes, open the jar. You will see whipped cream. Keep shaking for five to ten more minutes.

④ Check your cream. A hard lump will form. That lump is butter. The white liquid around it is buttermilk.

⑤ Pour out the buttermilk. (You can save this and use it for another recipe, if you like.)

⑥ Put your butter into a bowl. Pour cold water over it to rinse it off. Then, pour off the water.

⑦ With your hands, shape your butter into a ball. Your butter is ready to serve. Yum!

GLOSSARY

brands: Names that identify products or the companies that make them.

canned: Placed and preserved in a sealed can.

colonial: Of or having to do with the people who formed the original 13 colonies of the United States.

cultures: The ideas, customs, traditions, and ways of life of groups of people.

delis: Stores that sell prepared foods, such as salads and sliced meats and cheeses.

electricity: Electrical power that is generated in special plants and distributed to all parts of the country.

gourmet: Fancy or complicated food or cooking.

icebox: A box or chest kept cool with blocks of ice.

immigrants: People who leave their home countries to live in a new country.

organic: Grown without artificial chemicals or fertilizers.

preserve: To treat food in different ways so that it does not spoil.

processed: Prepared or changed by a series of steps.

spoiled: Became rotten or unfit for eating.

INDEX

TO LEARN MORE

Finding more information is as easy as 1, 2, 3.

1 **Go to www.factsurfer.com**

2 **Enter "cookingthenandnow" into the search box.**

3 **Click the "Surf" button to see a list of websites.**

FACT SURFER